Leah Komaiko

SHOESHINE SHIRLEY

A Doubleday Book for Young Readers

illustrated by Franz Spohn

A Doubleday Book for Young Readers
Published by
Delacorte Press
Bantam Doubleday Dell Publishing Group, Inc.
1540 Broadway
New York, New York 10036

Doubleday and the portrayal of an anchor with a dolphin are trademarks of
Bantam Doubleday Dell Publishing Group, Inc.

Library of Congress Cataloging in Publication Data

Komaiko, Leah.
    Shoeshine Shirley / by Leah Komaiko ; illustrated by Franz Spohn.
        p.   cm.
    Summary: There are all kinds of shoes in her shop, and Shoeshine Shirley knows
whose are whose.
    ISBN 0-385-30526-5
    [1. Shoes—Fiction.   2. Stories in rhyme.]   I. Spohn, Franz, ill.
II. Title.
PZ8.3.K835Sh   1993   [E]—dc20   92-25816   CIP   AC

Manufactured in the United States of America
September 1993
10 9 8 7 6 5 4 3 2 1

For Bird, Tim, and Shirley's mentor, Valerie Lewis
—L.K.

For Gina, Sarah, Elise, and Jessica
—F.S.

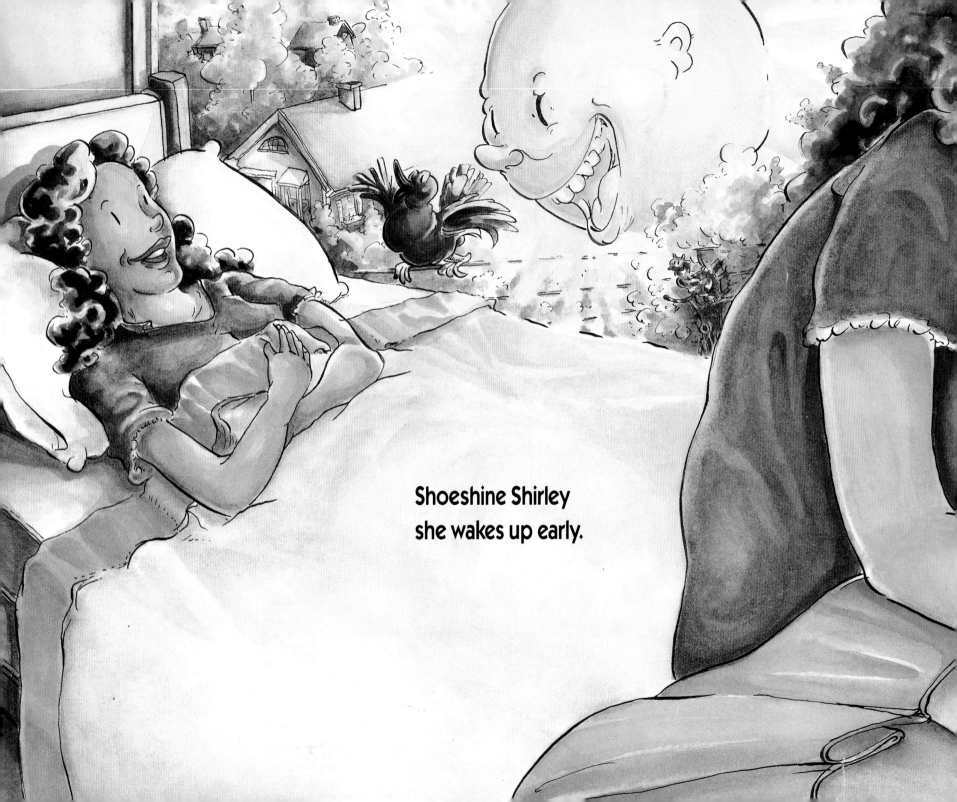

Shoeshine Shirley
she wakes up early.

She takes her shoes out and says, "**Rise and shine!**"

She buffs up her best fruit
and zips up her work suit.
There's a line down there
at her shoe repair
by a quarter to nine....

Row after shelf
after row of old shoes.
How does Shoeshine Shirley
know
whose are whose?

She knows
whose shoes
stack the news,

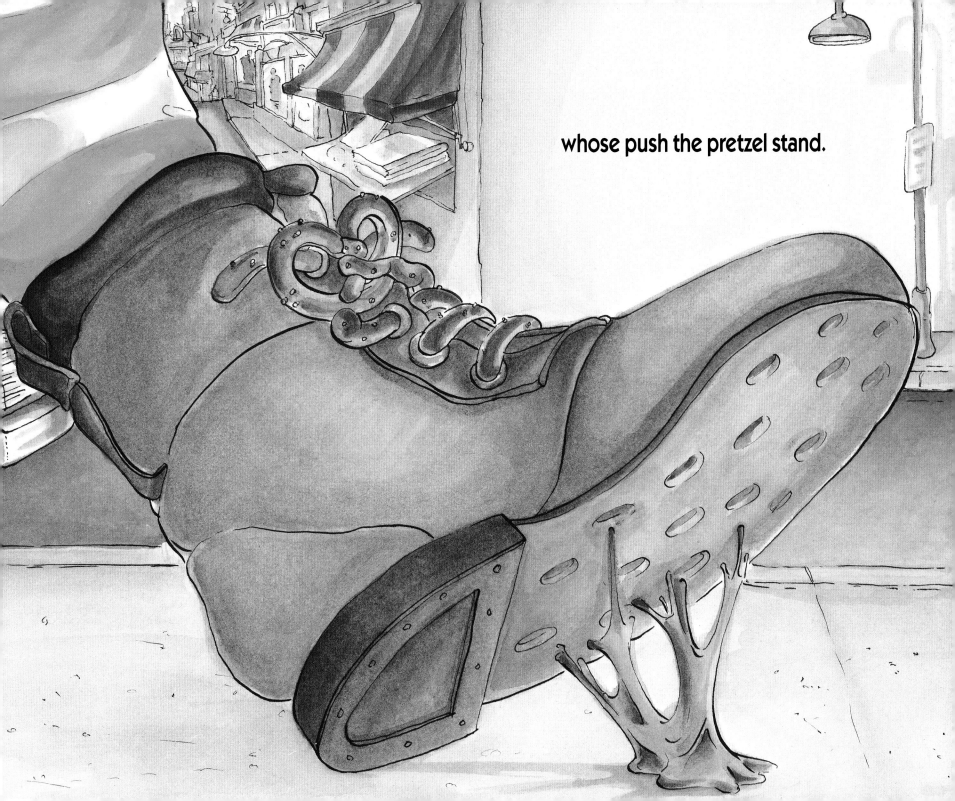

whose push the pretzel stand.

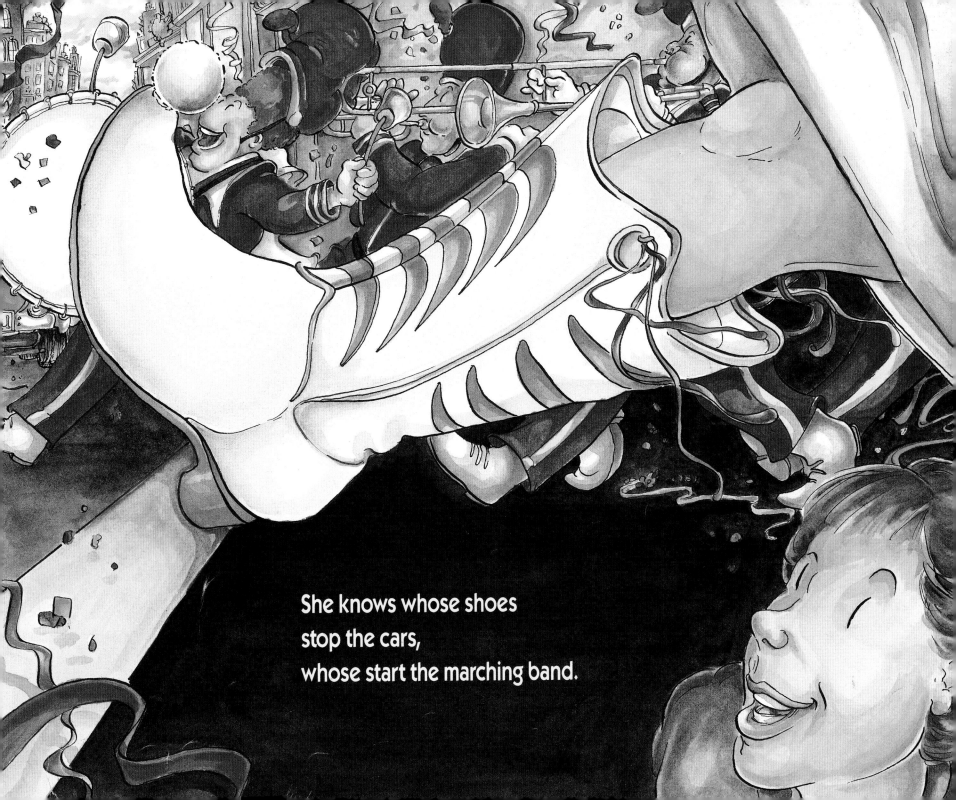

She knows whose shoes
stop the cars,
whose start the marching band.

"I shine the shoes
  that look sickly.
  Their tongues are green and prickly.
  The laces
  left their places.

They ran OUT OF HERE."

She knows whose shoes
raise the flag,

whose open up the store.

She knows whose shoes
sweep the street,

whose dust the dinosaur.

"I know whose shoes
stuck together.
They slept out in bad weather.
They're here for Shirley's
shining,

She knows whose shoes
rent canoes,

whose give rides in the street.

She knows whose shoes

kick the ball,

whose go to baby feet.

"I know whose shoes
should be walking
(those toes weren't made for talking),

whose shoes are so lonely—
why must they be the only
ones stuck inside a brown sack?
The owner never came back.
Won't someone help them, please?

LEAH KOMAIKO is the author of many books for children, including *Aunt Elaine Does the Dance from Spain* and *Broadway Banjo Bill*. Leah Komaiko was born in Chicago and has lived most of her life in big cities because, she says, they have good shoe-repair shops. When she is not writing books for children she travels to speak at schools across the country. She is also writing her first book for adults.

FRANZ SPOHN is an illustrator, an artist, a printmaker, and a sculptor who has exhibited his work in museums throughout the United States and Canada. The American Craft Museum in New York City showed an exhibition that included his mosaic sculptures made of cupcake sprinkles. At one time Franz Spohn was known as Yikes the Clown. He holds BFA and MFA degrees from Ohio State University, Columbus. Franz Spohn illustrated *Broadway Banjo Bill* by Leah Komaiko. He is currently working on an unusual alphabet book.

The illustrations were done with Hunt Speedball pen nibs 22B and 104 using technical black india ink with Winsor & Newton watercolors on Strathmore archival two-ply hot-press bristol board. The text of the book is set in 20-, 24-, 28-, and 36-point Kabel with 36-point Kabel Contour for display. Typography by Lynn Braswell.